KT-476-855

£6.99

MORE NAUTICAL NARRATIVE ANON!

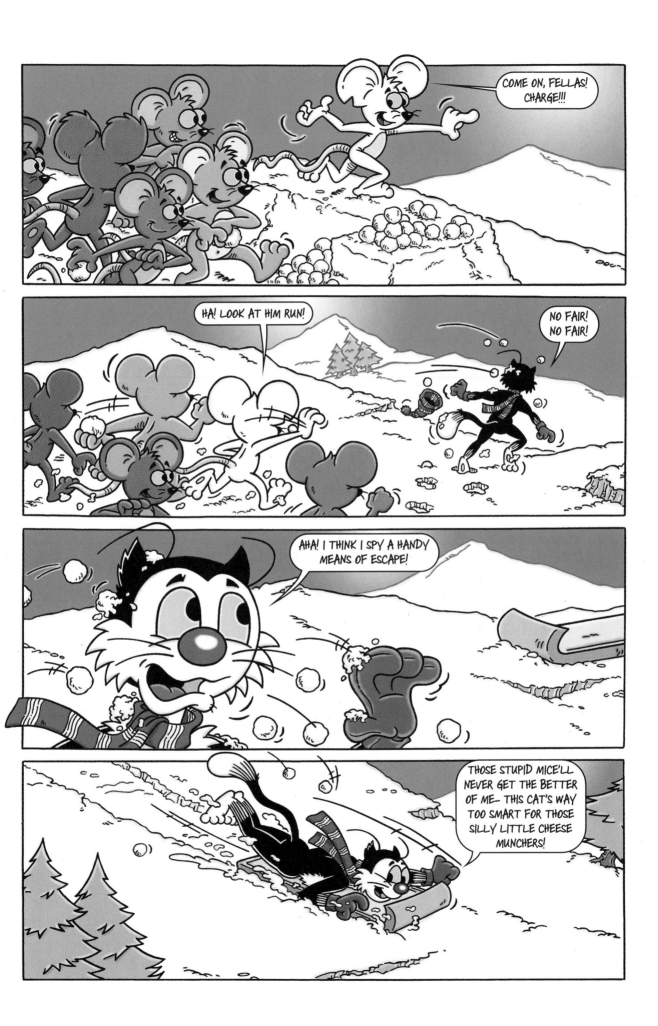

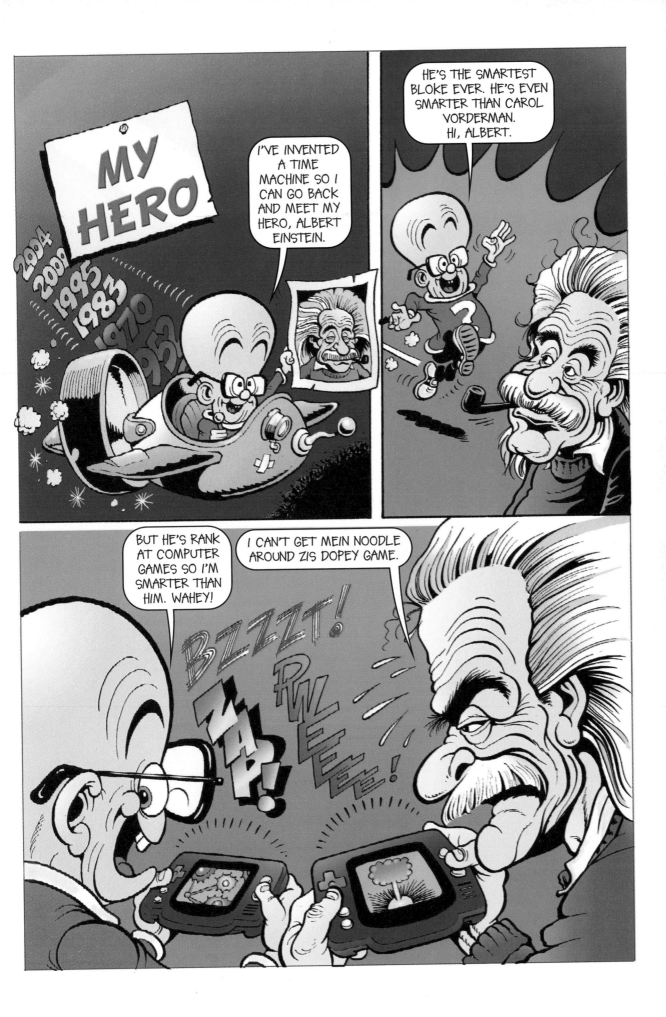

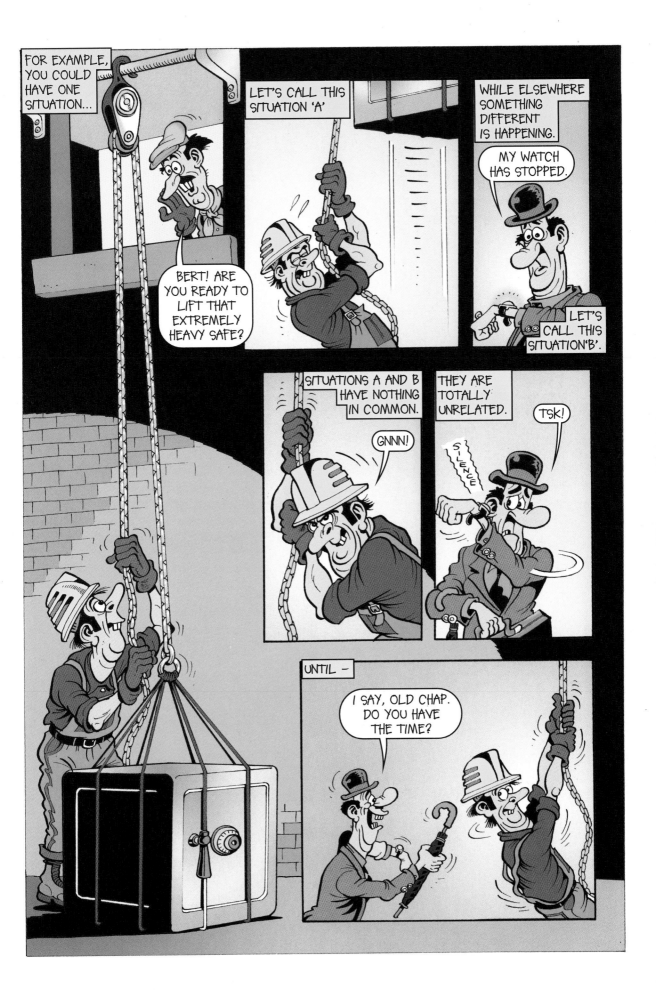

KEYHOLE KATE

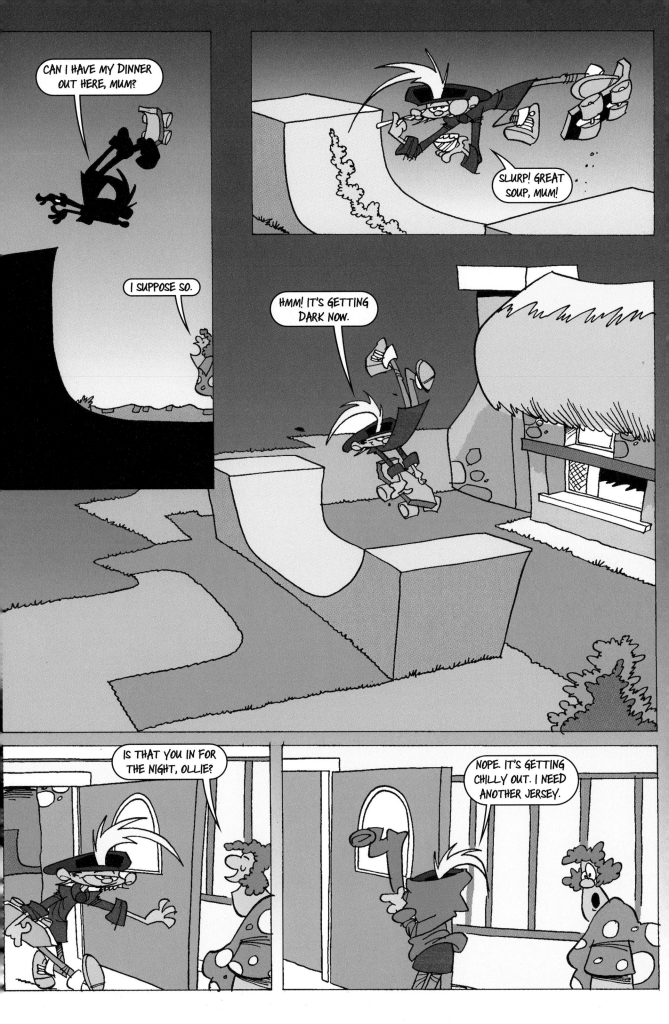

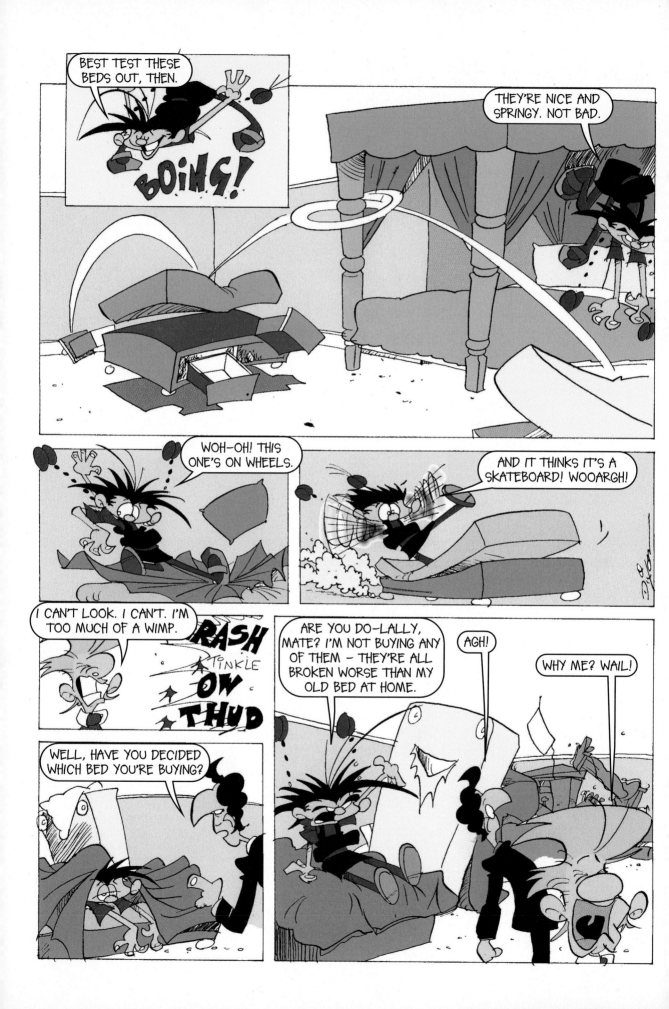

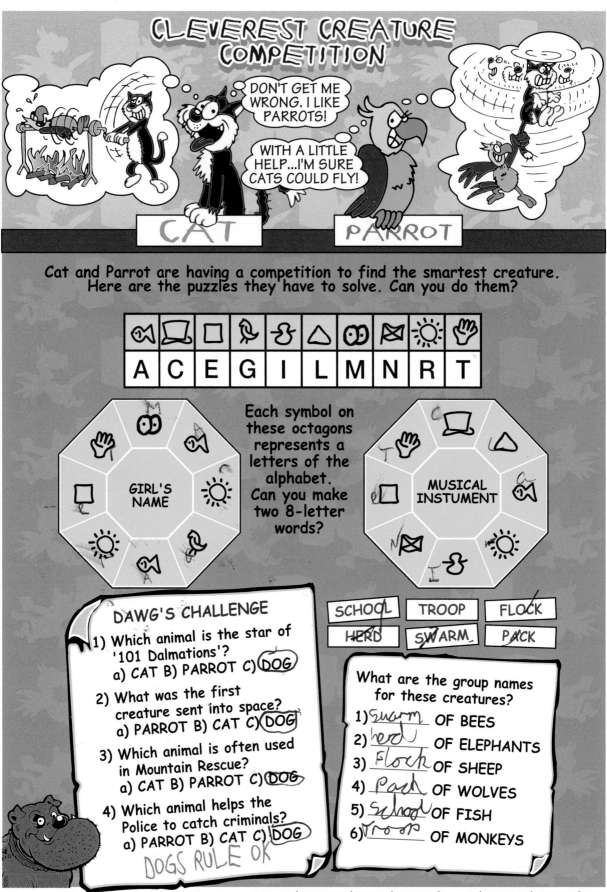

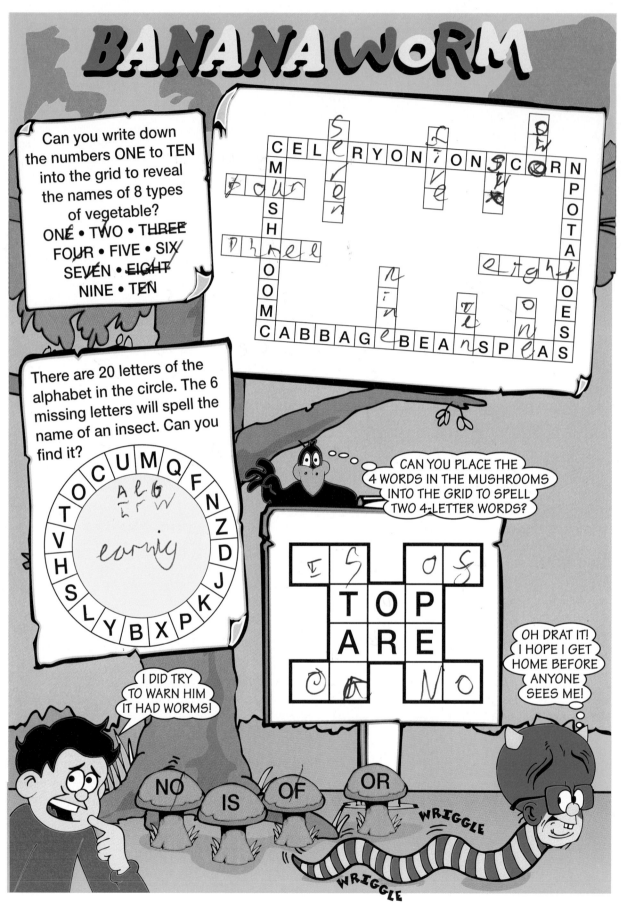

BANANA WORM

Can you write down the numbers ONE to TEN into the grid to reveal the names of 8 types of vegetable?
ONE • TWO • THREE
FOUR • FIVE • SIX
SEVEN • EIGHT
NINE • TEN

There are 20 letters of the alphabet in the circle. The 6 missing letters will spell the name of an insect. Can you find it?

CAN YOU PLACE THE 4 WORDS IN THE MUSHROOMS INTO THE GRID TO SPELL TWO 4-LETTER WORDS?

I DID TRY TO WARN HIM IT HAD WORMS!

OH DRAT IT! I HOPE I GET HOME BEFORE ANYONE SEES ME!

NO   IS   OF   OR

WRIGGLE
WRIGGLE

DAN/14-04
Gall & Strachan

BANANA DUANE

1 ACROSS IS 'BIG DIPPER'!

MINI CROSSWORD

CLUES ACROSS
1) Funfair ride (3,6)
5) A rodent (3)
6) Writing fluid (3)
7) Very keen (5)

CLUES DOWN
1) Dog sound (4)
2) Field entrance (4)
3) Two cards the same (4)
4) Garden tool (4)

CAN YOU SPOT 8 DIFFERENCES BETWEEN DUANE'S THOUGHT BUBBLES?

IT'S BANANADUANE!

IT'S BANANADUANE!

MUNCH! MUNCH! MUNCH!

TOO LATE ERIC! I'M ABOUT TO BECOME BANANA...

DON'T EAT THAT BANANA DUANE!

DAN/13-04
Gall & Strachan

Answers: Crossword Across 1) BIG DIPPER 5) RAT 6) INK 7) EAGER. Down 1) BARK 2) GATE 3) PAIR 4) RAKE.
Spot the Difference 1) BIRDS 2) SWINGS 3) BANANADUANE'S LEG 4) TREES 5) WINDOW 6) PEOPLE 7) CAR 8) CHIMNEY.

KEYHOLE KATE

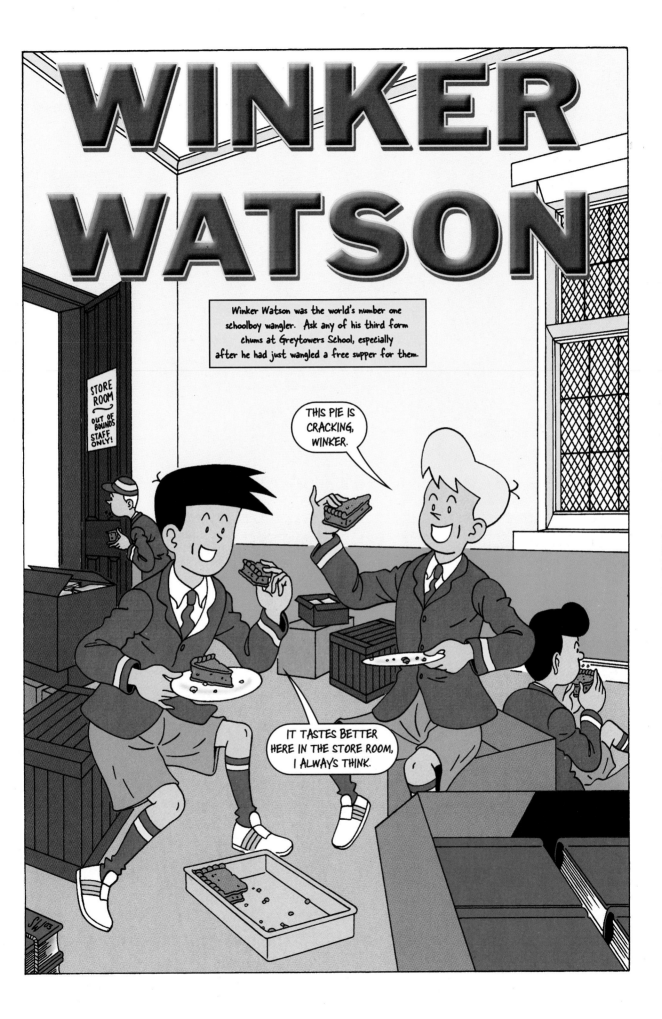

Soon —

WATSON, MR CREEP IS LOCKED IN THE STORE. HURRY ALONG TO THE JANITOR AND GET HIS SKELETON KEYS.

STORE ROOM
OUT OF BOUNDS STAFF ONLY!

Then —

MR CREEP — YOUR FACE IS COVERED IN TART — HAVE YOU BEEN HAVING A FEAST IN THERE?

The janitor's keys had given Winker an idea. He zipped off to see some students he knew.

MEDICAL SCHOOL HALL OF RESIDE

SURE WE'LL HELP, WINKER. WAIT AND I'LL MAKE IT UP INTO PARCELS FOR YOU.

THERE YOU GO.

TA, I'LL TAKE GOOD CARE OF IT.

HMM! DOGS FOLLOWING TROTT? VERY SUSPICIOUS. YOU, BOY — STOP!

I'M CONFISCATING THAT PARCEL YOU'RE HOLDING.

IT'S NOTHING, SIR.